ZULEIKA
IN
CAMBRIDGE

S. C. Roberts

OLEANDER PRESS

The Oleander Press
16 Orchard Street
Cambridge
CB1 1JT

www.oleanderpress.com

First published by Heffer & Sons: 1941
This edition published by The Oleander Press: August 2009
This edition © 2009. All rights reserved.

The publisher has made every effort to establish whether any party holds the original copyright to this work. Any person or institution believing they have an interest in the rights are invited to contact the publisher at the address shown.

No part of this publication may be reproduced, stored in a retrieval system, or transmitted, in any form or by any means without the prior permission in writing of the publisher, nor be otherwise circulated in any form of binding or cover other than in which it is published and without a similar condition including this condition being imposed on the subsequent purchaser.

A CIP catalogue record for the book is available from the British Library.

ISBN: 9780906672976

Designed and typeset by Hamish Symington
www.hamishsymington.com

Printed in England

"See if it is possible to go direct from here to Cambridge," said Zuleika... "Stop!" she said suddenly. "I have a much better idea. Go down very early to the station. See the station-master. Order me a special train..."

           Max Beerbohm, *Zuleika Dobson*

I

THE SPECIAL TRAIN WHICH Zuleika had instructed Mélisande to order for ten o'clock on the morning following the annihilating tragedy of Eights Week did not start punctually. The station-master was not prepared to accept the order as a matter of the day's routine. Of course he had arranged special trains before; there had been a year when he had facilitated the departure of a Royal Personage returning from the glories of the Encaenia and a pair of cuff-links engraved with the august monogram remained, unworn, in its case on his drawing-room table. But a peremptory order from a young woman given at 8.30 in the morning in a suspiciously foreign accent was unprecedented.

"Who's the train for?" asked the station-master with ungrammatical directness.

"For Miss Dobson."

"Never heard of her."

"You never hear of Miss Dobson, Miss Zuleika Dobson! But she is the grand-daughter of the Warden of Judas College, yes."

At this the station-master showed some interest. He took the precaution, however, of consulting the Proctor by telephone. The Proctor replied, feverishly, that the sooner Miss Dobson left Oxford, the better. When he heard that her destination was Cambridge, his enthusiasm rose still higher.

So Zuleika's train was prepared and perhaps the Roman Emperors sighed wistfully. Lately they had seen so much – it had been like old times.

Slowly the special train passed through the cavalier country and approached the puritan plains of East Anglia.

Zuleika's spirits drooped. She knew little of English history, but by some premonition she was aware that the country in which a Knight of the Garter would die for an idea was receding from her... Could it be, she wondered, that she was being guilty of an impossible disloyalty?

At Bletchley there was some delay. Special or no special, it was too much to expect that the train should pass every signal-box unchallenged. Zuleika fumed and Mélisande still showed a tendency to sulk.

At length the train drew up at the Cambridge platform. Already, it appeared, several other trains – ordinary trains – were halted at it; but as the platform stretched far, far beyond the limits of human vision, it seemed to matter little – except to Zuleika. Why had not Mélisande arranged things better?

"But, mademoiselle, I order a special train where we begin. I could order not a special *voie* where we finish."

"We are not finishing," said Zuleika, "we are beginning again."

Alas, there was no Warden to meet Zuleika at the station. In Cambridge, of course, they do not have

Wardens, but Zuleika could not know that. But at least there were porters and Mélisande quickly secured, and fully employed, three of them. The cab-rank was, to Zuleika, uninviting, but a hansom for herself, another for Mélisande and the light luggage, and two others for the heavy luggage proved to be an adequate, if not very convenient, means of transport.

"Where to, Miss?" enquired the leading cabman.

To this Zuleika was unable to give a ready answer. She had, so far as she knew, no relatives or friends in Cambridge. But Cambridge, she assumed, had, like Oxford, a number of colleges. Did the grand-daughter of the head of an Oxford college acquire any status, by affiliation or otherwise, in Cambridge? It was long before the days of "friendly alliances" between Oxford and Cambridge colleges and Zuleika was puzzled.

"Which is the best college?" she asked the cabman.

"That's not for me to say, Miss. Of course, some's better class than others, but nowadays there's all sorts in most of 'em. Now if you just tell me which one your brother or friend is in, I'll take you there."

But Zuleika, alas, could not.

"Are there hotels?" she asked.

"Yes, plenty, Miss."

"Take me to the best."

"Very good, Miss."

So the cavalcade set off.

The first part of the journey did not impress, or amuse, Zuleika. The Station Road was like all Station Roads in the world – perhaps more so, since when the railway had first come to Cambridge, it had been the particular care of the University authorities to remove its distracting influence as far as possible from the centre of academic calm. A one-horse tram, which occasionally interfered with the orderly sequence of the four hansoms, seemed to be the only distinguishing feature of Cambridge transport. Even when the cabs swung round into another street, Zuleika could see no evidence of collegiate grandeur. No Roman Emperors looked down upon her, though shortly an imposing spire came into view. Zuleika surmised that it might be the cathedral. How could she know that it was but a modern church, alien alike from Anglican and Cantabrigian tradition? The hansoms swung to the left and passed a row of villas which might well have reminded Zuleika of Oxford had her knowledge of that city extended to its northern area and not been confined to Judas College and the meadows.

But the last swerve of the cab brought her to something better – a street of gentle but repeated curves with solid terraced houses, a running stream in each gutter and, later, a jumble of shops and colleges.

Just as Zuleika was contemplating this medley, the hansoms drew up alongside the hotel. Mélisande dealt with the four cabmen while Zuleika issued an order for the best suite available. The bathroom arrangements seemed to her inadequate, but she supposed that they must suffice – at least until she should be able to establish herself under a more dignified and appropriate roof. Meanwhile she was hungry. It was after two o'clock and as she approached the dining-room, she saw that it was empty, save for a young man who was lingering over his coffee. Zuleika inferred that he was an undergraduate, though probably not a duke. Nevertheless, a slight thrill shot through her tired frame. It was a meeting not comparable with her initial encounter with the Duke of

Dorset, but here was Zuleika face to face for the first time with a Cambridge undergraduate; and undergraduates, she assumed (as Dr Johnson assumed of the waters of the sea), were much the same everywhere. She hoped that the young man would not fall in love with her too violently before she had had her lunch.

As she entered the room, the victim, as it seemed, leapt violently to his doom.

"Ah, at last you've come."

Zuleika recognised the tone. It was a lover's welcome. So, she mused, it was inevitable. The greeting was freer, gayer, less dignified, perhaps; but the magic was still working. Quickly Zuleika began to speculate on the probable course of events. Had they a river at Cambridge? Yes, she thought she had heard of Cambridge boating and boat-races, but what was the capacity of the Cambridge river? What of the reeds and mud to which she had heard vaguely scornful reference made in Oxford? If young men must die for her, she liked them to die cleanly... Her reverie was harshly interrupted.

"Oh, I beg your pardon," said the young man, "I'm frightfully sorry... I thought you were – "

"You thought I was – ?" murmured Zuleika.

"I thought you were my – er – friend. You see, I was just waiting for her and – well, here she is. I'm awfully sorry."

The friend had round blue eyes and fluffy fair hair. Zuleika sat down to her lunch.

II

SIPPING HER *CAFÉ NOIR*, Zuleika reviewed the situation. The encounter with the young man was puzzling. Yet it might well be that he was not an undergraduate; possibly he was just a visitor passing through the town. The hotel seemed now to be empty except for two elderly ladies dozing over illustrated papers in the lounge. Zuleika was wondering how to approach the problem of Cambridge. With no grandfather and, so far, no duke to guide or shelter her, she found it difficult. But at least the sun was shining and she stepped out into the street.

The pinnacles of King's were silhouetted against the cerulean blue of the summer sky and Zuleika contemplated them with quizzical awe. So far as she could remember, she had seen nothing quite like them in Oxford. But she had not come to Cambridge to contemplate pinnacles. How, she reflected, was she to make acquaintance with a Cambridge college from within? At that moment the hotel-porter approached her.

"You're wanted, please, Miss," he said.

"By whom?"

"It's the manager, Miss. I think he's got a message for you."

Zuleika turned back into the hotel. The manager seemed to be slightly perturbed.

"I'm sorry to trouble you, Miss Dobson," he said politely, "but the Senior Proctor wishes to see you at once."

"What is a Proctor?" asked Zuleika. "Is it the same as a Warden?"

The question confused the manager a little. The only kind of warden with which he was familiar was a church-warden. He knew, of course, that the Proctors attended divine service, compulsorily, on certain occasions; but he rightly associated them with disciplinary, rather than with spiritual, responsibility.

"The Proctors," he said, "keep an eye on the undergraduates."

Zuleika brightened at this.

"I see," she said, "and what is the message?"

The manager read from a piece of paper:

"The Senior Proctor presents his compliments to Miss Dobson and would be obliged if she would call upon him in his rooms at her earliest convenience."

"Why doesn't he call upon me?" asked Zuleika.

"I expect it's easier to talk privately in his rooms," said the manager tactfully.

Zuleika was mollified. The message was not rapturous, but it was polite and would at least give her contact with a university personage.

"Where does the Proctor live?" she asked.

"In St Benedict's."

"Then order a cab."

"But, excuse me, Miss Dobson. St Benedict's is only just across the road."

"Oh very well, but it is tiring to walk across roads in the strong sunshine. Where is Mélisande?"

On the subject of proctors Mélisande was not helpful. If they bore any resemblance to a *procurateur*, she recommended avoidance.

Zuleika crossed the road and found herself at the main gate of the college of St Benedict. A dignified porter, wearing a silk hat, looked at her with the half-suspicious, half-tolerant expression with which he greeted all May Term visitors.

"The Proctor wishes to see me," said Zuleika simply.

"You mean Mr Mackenzie, Miss. K Old Court."

Zuleika was not enlightened. The description reminded her vaguely of a move at chess.

"Through the screens, Miss," said the porter helpfully. But still Zuleika was at a loss. The porter realised that he had to deal with the really hopeless May Term type. He walked far enough with Zuleika to show her the precise approach to Mr Mackenzie's staircase.

Brian Mackenzie, formerly of the University of Aberdeen, and now Fellow and Mathematical Lecturer of St Benedict's and Senior Proctor in the University, was a man of tidy mind and tidy habits. He had no love of the office of Proctor, but he had recognised the obligation to serve and he had come through the greater part of his year of office without any major scandal or disturbance. He had a reputation for courtesy, dignity and efficiency.

What he had heard from Oxford in the preceding twenty-four hours had filled him with incredulous astonishment. He had been convinced that the daily press, following its invariable practice of putting Oxford in the headlines and Cambridge in the University Intelligence, had grossly exaggerated the devastation produced by the visit of Zuleika to Judas College. Nevertheless, when the news of her migration to Cambridge reached him, he felt that he must act and act promptly. He had called upon the Vice-Chancellor and suggested that he should summon a special meeting of the Proctorial Syndicate. The Vice-Chancellor was disturbed. As Full Term drew to an end, he liked to resume his collation of certain Syriac fragments which seemed to embody a dialect hitherto unknown to scholars and he hoped shortly to complete an article on the subject for

The Journal of Oriental Studies. He, too, had heard something about strange happenings at the other university, but when he had caught sight of a headline "Oxford Sensation" he had shuddered slightly and put the newspaper down. The description of an event as a "sensation" always produced in him a feeling of incipient nausea. However, he trusted Mackenzie's judgement and a meeting of the Proctorial Syndicate had been convened for five o'clock.

Mackenzie's aim was clear. He wanted to remove Zuleika from Cambridge as quickly and as quietly as possible. Sceptical as he was about the measure of disaster which she had brought upon Oxford, he desired above all things to see her safely in a Liverpool Street train. It was a policy he had pursued with some success, during his year of office, in relation to female immigrants of a different type. "Let us have a minimum of fuss," he used to say at proctorial conferences. As a mathematician, Mackenzie had a reputation for neatness rather than for elegance.

He rose to greet Zuleika.

"Ah, Miss Dobson, this is very kind of you. Won't you sit down?"

Zuleika sat down slowly and looked round the room, at its bookshelves heavy with treatises on Octonions and Invariants and Periodic Functions and Sets of Points and Twisted Cubics, all in massive dark blue bindings; at the mantelpiece with its neat array of pipes and fixture-cards; at the pile of *Proceedings* of the London Mathematical Society on a side table; at the faded Persian hearth-rug and the deep padded chairs on each side of it.

"So you are the Proctor," said Zuleika.

"I am."

"You sent for me. Why do you want me?"

"I wished to have a talk with you."

"And you could not brook delay?"

"Miss Dobson, it was important that I should have an opportunity of speaking to you and, in particular, that I should take the opportunity before five o'clock this afternoon."

"So soon? Do you wish to die for me at five o'clock?"

Mackenzie was irritated. Either the girl was a lunatic or she was trying to make a fool of him. In either case she was wasting time.

"I have no wish," he began, "to enter into unnecessary detail. But as an official of the University responsible for the discipline and good behaviour of undergraduates – "

"Oxford undergraduates behave divinely."

"Outside Cambridge I have no jurisdiction," said Mackenzie a little sharply.

"Has the college ghost walked?" asked Zuleika.

Mackenzie was for a moment thrown out of his official stride. In any other college the question might have been disregarded as a piece of frivolous irrelevance. But the St Benedict's ghost was famous. It was the only one which had crept into the guidebooks.

"An ancient college like this accumulates much curious tradition," said Mackenzie, temporising.

"Will it walk at five o'clock?" asked Zuleika, disregarding the generalisation.

"I have never seen it," said Mackenzie curtly.

"And did the black owls perch on the battlements last night, hooting until the dawn?"

Again, Mackenzie was unfortunate. The owls which favoured the elm trees within the precincts of the college on the opposite side of the street were becoming an intolerable nuisance to light sleepers in St Benedict's. At a recent college meeting Mackenzie had urged that a strong letter of protest should be addressed to the governing body of the offending college.

"May we not return to the subject of our discussion?" he said politely.

"But what is the subject?" asked Zuleika.

"In a word – yourself," said Mackenzie with great suavity.

"At Oxford they did not summon me to discussions. They just died for me. Do *you* wish to die for me – at five o'clock?"

"For that hour, my dear Miss Dobson, I already have a more vital engagement. The Vice-Chancellor has agreed to preside over a special meeting of the Proctorial Syndicate."

"What is this meeting for?"

Mackenzie took up a piece of paper from his writing-table.

"The draft of the terms of reference which I have ventured to propose to the Vice-Chancellor is here. I will read it to you: 'To consider the steps to be taken to meet the situation arising out of the arrival in Cambridge of a stranger alleged to have caused grave disturbance in another university.' That, of course, is a draft and subject to amendment. But it may serve to show that the University is likely to take a serious view."

"But aren't Universities always serious?" asked Zuleika humbly.

"The University has a variety of functions to perform," replied Mackenzie.

"And what does a Syndicate perform?"

"I have no wish to weary you, Miss Dobson, with the detail of academic procedure. But if I can inform the Vice-Chancellor and the Syndicate at five o'clock that you agree with the course I am about to propose – "

"You are about to propose?" repeated Zuleika with wide-open eyes.

"I am about to propose that you should leave Cambridge by the 6.25 train."

"But I have only just arrived."

"My dear Miss Dobson, I will refrain from the obvious retort, which no doubt would have been made in

Oxford, of the greater benefit of travelling hopefully. I have no wish to indulge in exaggerated censure, but in my position I am bound to safeguard the University against risk."

"Risk of what?"

"Risk of – er – disturbance of the undergraduate population."

Zuleika was growing weary. The conversation had taken on a staccato quality.

"Are you going to offer me tea?" she enquired.

Momentarily taken aback, Mackenzie made a quick recovery. He had no wide experience of negotiations with females, for, in Edwardian times, ladies did not sit upon Faculty Boards. But he knew that, just as valuable concessions in academic negotiation could be most successfully secured after the port had travelled twice round the table, so, with women, it was necessary to conduct really important business over the tea-cups.

Normally he did not take afternoon tea himself. His gyp did not report to him until 6 o'clock. It would be necessary for him to visit the buttery himself. "But, of course," he said amiably, "excuse me for a moment."

When he reached the buttery, he found the main door locked. He tried the side door to the butler's private room, but the room was empty. Shortly a buttery-boy, only recently engaged, appeared. Mackenzie stated his wants. The boy stated in reply that the buttery staff would "come on" in about ten minutes' time.

"I want tea for two and cakes – in my rooms at once," said Mackenzie.

"What sort of cakes?" asked the boy.

"Oh – the best sort," said Mackenzie.

"I'll tell them," said the boy. It was all he could do. Meanwhile Zuleika sat in Mackenzie's rooms. She was bored. She could not follow very clearly all the talk about Vice-Chancellors and Syndicates and she certainly did not intend to leave by the 6.25. She wanted to learn what Cambridge men were like and poor Mackenzie seemed to her to be not so much a man as a piece of official mechanism. A phrase came into her head. It had been spoken to her in her early days of struggle by an unsympathetic employer: "No good purpose will be served by prolonging this interview." Zuleika felt that it was apt. She went out.

"Find Mr Mackenzie all right, Miss?" said the porter cheerfully.

"Yes, thank you – and lost him."

III

ZULEIKA STOOD AT THE gate of St Benedict's and turned her steps towards the hotel. Then she changed her mind and turned in the opposite direction. The hotel held no attraction for her. Instead, she gazed wonderingly at a Gothic pile which faced her on the opposite side of the street. She was unable to determine whether it was a college or a church. There was no one to tell her that it was just a printing-house.

So she went on and came to a gateway which must surely betoken another college. Was it full of more

Mackenzies, she wondered. At that moment a young man came out of the college. He caught sight of Zuleika and stopped. A light of thrilled recognition came into his eye.

"Excuse me," he said, "but aren't you Miss Dobson, Miss Zuleika Dobson?"

Zuleika looked at the young man through her long lashes. Who could he be? Someone who had escaped from Oxford and followed her across? Or had he merely seen her picture in the illustrated papers. If so, his effrontery must be crushed.

"That is my name," she said, "but I do not think I have the pleasure – "

"Oh, of course, you wouldn't remember me. But you might conceivably remember giving a sort of semi-private show at the Jacobean Club at Yale last year. I was living at Yale at the same time and shook hands with you after the show. But of course you don't remember. Why should you?"

"Why should you remember me?"

"Because... well, you're Zuleika Dobson and I'm just Desmond Hawkins of Valence Hall."

"Are you a Proctor?"

Hawkins burst into laughter.

"Heavens, no! I've just come back for a fifth year, trying to write a thesis for a fellowship, you know."

But Zuleika didn't know anything about fellowship theses.

"Five years seems a long time," she said, "I haven't been in Cambridge for five hours yet."

"Where are you staying?"

"I'm not sure that I am staying. They want to send me away by the 6.25 train."

"Who wants to?"

"The Syndicate."

"What Syndicate?"

"I don't know," said Zuleika wearily. "I don't know anything about Cambridge. It seems so different from – "

"Yes, I know what you're going to say. It *is* different, I know. But, Miss Dobson, do tell me. There's an absurd rumour going round about everyone at Oxford dying for you. I suppose it's just another Oxford legend written up by some clever journalist. Do tell me about it."

Zuleika looked in some astonishment at the amused,

enquiring, and ingenuous countenance of Desmond Hawkins. He was recovering from his initial shyness and was now nearly at his ease. It was evident that he admired her, but it was equally evident that he did not believe in the Oxford stories. He was polite and charming, but he was not prostrate before her.

"Oxford indeed has died for me," she said in the voice of a tragedy-queen, "in Cambridge I am dying for a cup of tea."

Hawkins was startled. Had the fierce afternoon sunshine been too much for Zuleika? Or was she merely thirsty?

"Miss Dobson," he said eagerly, "if you'd really do me the honour of having tea in my rooms, I should be proud, of course, and delighted."

"Lead me to them," said Zuleika.

They went over the cobbles, which Zuleika disliked very much, and turned into a tiny cloister. Hawkins led the way up a narrow staircase and Zuleika followed him. She found herself in an untidy, but cosy room. There were several comfortable chairs. One of them was burdened with a pile of books, another with a tennis racket, another with a pair of flannel trousers, which Hawkins flung hastily into his bedroom.

Zuleika sank into the chair thus disencumbered.

"This is grand," said Hawkins.

Whatever other qualities the scene might hold, Zuleika felt that the element of grandeur was lacking.

"What is grand?" she murmured.

"Why, being able to persuade you to come and have tea with me like this."

"Like what?"

"Well, informally and... (Hawkins blushed slightly) alone."

"Then you are not afraid?"

"Afraid? Oh, you're harking back to that Oxford rumour? No, I'm sorry, Miss Dobson, but candidly I don't feel a bit like dying. I'd much rather go on living and – "

"And – ?" Zuleika's lips were parted.

"And get you some tea."

Zuleika sank back into the chair.

"That," she said, "would be a very admirable thing to do."

Hawkins began operations upon his Primus stove. It was, fortunately, in good order.

"If you don't mind waiting for half a minute, I'll just pop across to the buttery and get something to eat."

For the second time in half an hour Zuleika was left alone in college rooms. This time she had no desire to escape. Her host offered little of excitement or romance, but at least he did not talk gibberish about syndicates and terms of reference.

Hawkins re-appeared in a few minutes. He had given some quite precise orders about the food to be sent to his rooms. In particular he had made certain that the toast should be what was known in the college as "fellows' toast," neat little crustless triangles with just the right amount of butter evenly spread, not the solid slabs moistened in the middle which were commonly served to undergraduates. Also he made a point of ordering a few slices of lemon.

"Ah, the kettle is nearly boiling," he said cheerfully. "As it happens, I have some China tea. You'd prefer that, wouldn't you?"

"Yes, I think I should."

"And you also prefer a slice of lemon to milk?"

"Yes. Don't you?"

"No, I can't stand it, but I felt sure you would."

"Why?"

"Well, you're that sort."

"What sort?"

"Well, shall we say, a little... exotic?"

"And what precisely does the word 'exotic' signify?"

"Oh, I say, you mustn't press me too hard. Anyhow, it's the opposite of 'dowdy.'"

"I am relieved," said Zuleika, "to find that I am not dowdy."

The kettle boiled, Hawkins made the tea, and a buttery-boy entered with a number of dishes.

"What will you have to eat? Toast?" asked Hawkins.

"A tiny piece," said Zuleika. But in fact she ate four.

"How about a sandwich now?" said Hawkins.

"A sandwich?" cried Zuleika, visualising the crude layers of ham dear to masculine appetite.

"Oh, come," said Hawkins, "these are really rather tasty." He held before her a plate of diminutive confections at the heart of which was Gentleman's Relish or, alternatively, *pâté de foie gras.*

"Or there are these little things if you prefer them," Hawkins went on, indicating coffee éclairs of small size but agreeable texture.

Zuleika made a triple surrender.

"To take tea with you, Mr Hawkins," she said, "is an agreeable experience, but to repeat it would be to ruin my figure."

"I don't believe it, Miss Dobson – , I mean about your figure. But it's been wonderful to be able to entertain you for a few minutes like this."

Zuleika rose.

"Can I escort you anywhere, Miss Dobson? I expect you may want to rest a bit. No doubt you have a lot of engagements here."

"I know no one in Cambridge," said Zuleika.

"No one? Then why – "

"Why indeed did I come to Cambridge? Yes, you are entitled to ask that. They did wonderful things for me in Oxford, but in retrospect I cannot help feeling that they overdid them. The art of dying for me ceased, I fear, to be an art. It degenerated into a stampede. Nothing, as they say in Oxford, impedes like excess."

"D'you really mean, Miss Dobson, that you're free of engagements for this evening, for instance?"

"I am free of everything except my memories," said Zuleika. "Up to now I have looked forward always, but now there is nothing left but retrospect."

"Then, if it isn't too bold on my part to suggest it, would you care to dine with me?"

"Here?" asked Zuleika.

"Well, no. You see, my rooms are not really large enough for a party, but to-night, as it happens, Duxberry (one of the younger dons here) and his wife and a few others are dining with me in the Guest Room and after dinner we're going to move across to another man's rooms. Quite a friendly and informal affair. No fuss. It would be wonderful if you could join us."

Zuleika looked across at Hawkins. His enthusiasm was obvious, but it was the enthusiasm of youth in anticipation of a good lark. She reflected quietly which frock in her wardrobe would most suitably accord with the atmosphere of "no fuss." The dove-grey, perhaps? Or should she heighten the effect by wearing the flame-coloured dress with...? But suddenly she realised that she was choosing her dress before she had decided whether to accept the invitation.

"But your party, surely, is made up?" she temporised.

"It *was*. But it will be eternally incomplete unless – "

"I will come," said Zuleika.

IV

WHEN MACKENZIE RETURNED TO his rooms and found them empty, he was annoyed. He could not really believe that Zuleika was prowling around his bedroom, but he looked in to make sure and came to the conclusion, quite correctly, that Zuleika had quietly given him the slip. He hurried down to the porters' lodge.

"Has a lady just left the college, Barnicott?"

"Yes, Sir."

"Which way did she go?"

"Went along to the right, Sir."

For a moment Mackenzie thought of dashing off in pursuit, since it seemed clear that Zuleika had returned to her hotel. But he noted a rather curious look on the porter's face and refrained.

"Anything I can do, Sir?"

"Not at present, thank you, Barnicott. I may want to send a message later."

"Very good, Sir."

On his way back to his rooms Mackenzie remembered to cancel his order at the buttery.

It would, he reflected, be undignified to pursue Zuleika at the moment. Her disappearance suggested either that she was frightened or that she was up to some mischief. He confessed to himself that he thought the latter alternative more probable. However, he had at any rate succeeded in interviewing her and in giving her warning; he would be in a reasonably strong position at the meeting of the Proctorial Syndicate.

The Vice-Chancellor took the chair punctually, but with an air of mild grievance, at five o'clock.

He must apologise, he said, for summoning a meeting

of the Syndicate at such an unusual time and at such short notice. But circumstances of a peculiar nature had arisen which had given rise to grave apprehension in the mind of the Senior Proctor. Such apprehensions were due to reports, not at present wholly substantiated, of events of a somewhat alarming character which had occurred, or were alleged to have occurred, within the precincts of the sister university. In thus adumbrating the general situation the last thing he would wish to do would be to prejudge, in any particular, the issues which lay before the Syndicate. He would therefore call upon the Senior Proctor.

The Senior Proctor bowed slightly to the Vice-Chancellor and cleared his throat. He had no wish to take up the time of the Syndicate and would be as brief as possible. Information had reached him in the course of the morning concerning the recent visit of a Miss Zuleika Dobson to the University of Oxford – a lady rumoured, though he could with difficulty credit the rumour, to be closely related to one of the best known and most widely esteemed Heads of Houses in that university. Detailed reports, as the Vice-Chancellor had observed, were not at present forthcoming, but on the evidence available it appeared that the lady's influence among the junior members of the university had been of the most extraordinary and devastating character. After every allowance had been made for journalistic exaggeration it appeared tolerably certain that not a few undergraduate members of Oxford colleges, following the lead of a somewhat eccentric nobleman, had deliberately drowned themselves on account of this young woman.

"Don't believe a word of it!" interrupted Simpkins, a young classical don from Jesus, who was coaching one of his college boats and resented being dragged to the meeting at a most inconvenient hour.

Mackenzie, continuing, recognised that such an attitude of hasty incredulity could well be understood, but suggested that Mr Simpkins might suitably suspend judgement for the moment. The Syndicate, indeed, might feel at this point that however deeply they might commiserate with the sister university in her misfortune, the matter was officially no concern of theirs (*Hear, hear*). Unfortunately, it was impossible for the University to take up such a position of detachment.

Mackenzie paused. The Syndicate was listening to him now.

"I regret to have to inform the Syndicate," he concluded, "that the young lady in question is now in our midst."

"How do you know?" blurted Simpkins.

Mackenzie played his trump card.

"Because I interviewed her in my rooms two hours ago."

"Then why – " Simpkins began.

The Vice-Chancellor interposed.

"I am sure the Syndicate and indeed the University will be most grateful to the Senior Proctor for the great care and promptitude which he has shown in approaching this difficult problem. As to any further course of action to be followed, I am of course in the hands of the Syndicate."

"Could we be informed, Mr Vice-Chancellor, of our precise terms of reference?" asked the Vice-Master of Emmanuel.

The Vice-Chancellor looked a little perplexed, but Mackenzie promptly handed him a slip of paper.

"It is suggested," said the Vice-Chancellor, "that our business might be summarised in the following terms: 'To consider the steps to be taken to meet the situation arising out of the arrival in Cambridge of a stranger alleged to have caused grave disturbance in another university.'"

"Could the Senior Proctor tell us where the stranger is now?" asked Simpkins.

Mackenzie looked a little uncomfortable.

"She is staying at a hotel not far from my own college," he replied.

"Is she there now?"

"I believe so."

"Mr Vice-Chancellor," said Simpkins, "may we have this point cleared up a little? We know that two hours ago the lady was in the Senior Proctor's rooms. But where is she now? For all we know, while we are talking, she may be submerging freshmen right and left!"

"Mr Simpkins, please," said the Vice-Chancellor reproachfully.

"I have already made it clear," said Mackenzie, "that the lady is in all probability in her hotel."

"Probabilities," said the Junior Proctor, a logician from Sidney Sussex, "seem to be an unsatisfactory basis for a policy of action. But, assuming for the moment that the Proctors are successful in getting hold of the lady, may I enquire what we are to do with her?"

"Put her into the train for Liverpool Street," said Mackenzie.

"Under what Ordinance?" asked the Registrary, who had attended the meeting at the Vice-Chancellor's request.

"Surely the Proctors have summary powers in dealing with certain kinds of women?" said Mackenzie.

"This seems to be an uncertain kind," replied the Registrary tonelessly.

"Aren't we beating about the bush?" interposed Simpkins. "What I want to know is this: is the woman a bad lot or not?"

The Vice-Chancellor coughed.

"Perhaps," he said wanly, "the Senior Proctor would..." His voice faded.

"I really cannot undertake to give a categorical answer to Mr Simpkins' question," said Mackenzie.

"But you have talked to her in your own rooms, alone, haven't you?" retorted Simpkins.

Doctor Blenkinsop, Maitland Professor of Civil Law, spoke for the first time:

"With respect, Mr Vice-Chancellor, I venture to think the discussion has strayed a little from the main issue. While I would not suggest that the character of the lady is wholly irrelevant to the argument, it appears to me that there are two main questions to be determined: first, whether it is desirable that action should be taken to remove the lady from the precincts; and secondly, if the desirability of such action should be established, under what authority it should be taken. It is clearly not a case, in my submission, for the Sex Viri or for the Court of Discipline and, as at present advised, I should hesitate to subscribe to the view that the Proctors have any right of summary jurisdiction in such a case."

The Vice-Master of Emmanuel said that everything Professor Blenkinsop had said ought to be very carefully weighed. For his own part he was beginning to doubt whether the question before them could be satisfactorily examined by a body like the present Syndicate and, notwithstanding the very natural desire of the responsible officials to proceed without undue delay, he could not help wondering whether the most satisfactory course might not be the appointment of a small committee.

"A committee of this Syndicate or a body appointed *ad hoc*?" asked the Registrary.

"*Ad hoc* and *de novo*, I suggest," replied the Vice-Master, though he was at pains to add that he had not fully thought out the most appropriate constitution for the suggested committee.

"Mr Vice-Chancellor," said Greville of Trinity, who was sitting next to Simpkins and had had much whispered conversation with him, "may I with great respect enquire whether we are really getting anywhere?"

"I had understood," replied the Vice-Chancellor, "though of course I am open to correction by the Syndicate, I had understood that the Vice-Master of Emmanuel desired to formulate a motion. If such a motion should be seconded, perhaps Professor Blenkinsop might find it convenient to express his views in the form of an amendment."

But the Professor was understood to reply that, on reconsideration, he felt that, as major questions of academic policy might now be involved, it would be better to refer the whole question to the Council of the Senate.

"Mr Vice-Chancellor," Simpkins broke in, "if this matter is really urgent, can't we do something instead of just talking about committees?"

"Do I now understand," asked the Vice-Chancellor plaintively, "that the Vice-Master of Emmanuel's motion is not seconded?"

"In view of the turn the discussion has taken," replied the Vice-Master, "I am hardly prepared to make a formal motion."

"In that case," said Simpkins, "I beg to move that as the Senior Proctor has apparently caught the lady once and then let her slip through his fingers, he had better try again, with the aid of his bulldogs if necessary, and then tell us more about it."

"I second that," said Greville quickly.

"Mr Simpkins moves, and Mr Greville seconds, that... Perhaps the Registrary will give us the exact wording."

The Registrary read from his notes:

"That the Senior Proctor be requested to take immediate steps to gain further information, at first-hand, of a certain visitor; and to report to the Syndicate thereon."

"May I ask for a show of hands?" said the Vice-Chancellor.

Three hands went up.

"Those against?"

No hands were raised.

"Hardly a majority of the Syndicate, I am afraid," said the Vice-Chancellor sadly, "but nevertheless *nemine contradicente*. No doubt the Senior Proctor is now fully seized of the sense of the meeting, and I feel sure that he will very kindly undertake to report to us in due course. The Syndicate will adjourn."

V

ZULEIKA'S HANSOM DREW UP at the front gate of Valence Hall. Mélisande was with her, carrying a pair of goloshes (or, more accurately, overshoes) that had been a gift from a Rubber King after her final performance in Milwaukee. They were lined with swan's down and bore Zuleika's initials studded in diamonds. Mélisande slipped them over her mistress's shoes and accompanied her over the cobblestones to the foot of the staircase which led to the Guest Room.

After much reflection Zuleika had decided to wear a

dress of deep wine colour. It clung closely to her lithe figure and was wholly lacking in trimming or ornament. Amongst the May Term muslins its rich and sombre plainness produced a startling effect. Zuleika wore no jewelry save a snake-bracelet with deep ruby eyes. (It had been a parting tribute from the Maharajah of Kurrigalore.)

Hawkins greeted Zuleika with an air of subdued excitement, and introduced his other guests – Duxberry and his wife, Davidson (an undergraduate) and his sister, and a Newnham history don.

"I'll be frank with you, Miss Dobson," he said. "I had to get a man in a great hurry to make the party even. He's a bit late, I'm afraid, but he's coming all right."

Zuleika was not pleased. She had deliberately ordered her cab ten minutes late; she took no pleasure in making a penultimate entrance.

"Mr Simpkins, Sir," announced the gyp at the doorway.

"Ah, Simmy," said Hawkins, "that's splendid."

"Sorry I'm so late," said Simpkins, "but I've had to waste hours at a ridiculous meeting about some woman who's supposed to have – "

"May I introduce Miss Dobson," said Hawkins, quickly.

Simpkins gasped.

"Miss Zuleika Dobson?" he asked.

"Is it so strange a name?" said Zuleika.

"No, no. Not strange exactly. Just a little – what shall I say – coincidental."

They sat down. Zuleika was, of course, on the right of her host; on the other side of her was Simpkins. Inevitably Zuleika compared the scene in her mind's eye with her initial entertainment by the Warden of Judas. How different was the familiar gaiety of this party round the oval table from the superb and icy neglect with which the Duke had treated her at that first meeting. This was a party *sans cérémonie*, but, as the dinner progressed, Zuleika noted with satisfaction that there was no nonsense about "pot luck": the *vol-au-vent financière* was exquisite and the *crème brûlée* was something new in Zuleika's culinary experience.

Hawkins did not say much to Zuleika. In the first place he was conscious of his obligation to Mrs Duxberry whose chaperonage had facilitated the making of the party; also, the cares of the host were upon him and on this evening he felt that he had incurred no ordinary responsibilities. Further, he had a slight feeling of guilt, since, but for Zuleika's interruption, he would have had next to him Davidson's pretty sister. Zuleika, no doubt, would have been quick to observe something of this, had she not been continuously engaged in conversation by Simpkins.

Simpkins knew little more of Zuleika than what he had heard at the meeting of the Proctorial Syndicate; but this party was going to be the best joke of the term for him.

"D'you know Cambridge well, Miss Dobson?" he asked innocently.

"Can one know a place well in a few hours?"

"Hardly, perhaps. But people are more interesting than places, don't you think?"

"I am weary of both," said Zuleika, mournfully.

"Oh, come, Miss Dobson, don't judge us too hastily. People take their colour from places to some extent, I admit. In Oxford, for instance, a party like this might look very much the same at first glance, but in fact the people would be fundamentally different."

"I agree," said Zuleika, coldly.

"Oh, you know Oxford?" said Simpkins.

Hawkins had caught a little of this and broke in:

"You're barking up the wrong tree, Simmy. You can't teach Miss Dobson anything about Oxford."

The other little conversations round the table broke off. Simpkins was about to retort, but Duxberry slipped in a word from the end of the table.

"I hope," he said gallantly, "that we shan't try to teach Miss Dobson anything."

"The Warden of Judas is your grandfather, is he not, Miss Dobson?" said the Newnham don.

"He is," said Zuleika.

"A charming old gentleman, I believe," said Mrs Duxberry. "My brother-in-law stayed with him last term when he was preaching the University Sermon."

Simpkins was enjoying his second glass of Ruppertsberger.

"I daresay my conversational gambits are clumsy enough," he said, "but of course we all know that having devastated Oxford, Miss Dobson is now rapidly making us her slaves in Cambridge."

"Do you know the Senior Proctor?" asked Zuleika.

Simpkins laughed.

"Poor old Mac," he said. "Yes, you've captivated him."

"But he didn't seem to like me at all," said Zuleika. "He wanted to send me to Liverpool Street."

"He might at least have chosen King's Cross," said the Newnham don.

"Miss Dobson," said Hawkins, "I think what Mr Simpkins is trying to say is that we're all delighted to have you with us in Cambridge."

"I can say it much better than that," said Simpkins. "I'll give you a toast. The divine Zuleika and may we all live for ever to do her honour!"

The toast was drunk and they moved across to Davidson's rooms. To sit down in re-arranged pairs seemed something of an anti-climax.

"What do we do now?" said Simpkins, irrepressibly. "Sing? Dance? Play Consequences? Have you any parlour-tricks, Miss Dobson?"

For a moment Zuleika suspected a further attempt at leg-pulling. Furious, she gazed at Simpkins. Simpkins felt that he had never seen anyone half so beautiful. He even blushed, but Zuleika perceived that it was not a blush of shame. He was, in fact, unaware of Zuleika's professional activities and Zuleika, as she noted his rubicund adoration, knew that she had nothing to forgive. Why, after all, should she worry overmuch about young men dying for her if there were others with whom she could enjoy herself? Surprised, she heard herself saying:

"Let's play charades."

"Splendid," said Hawkins, much relieved.

"We're not a very large party," said Mrs Duxberry. "All you young people must act and Frank and I will be the audience."

The Newnham don brightened a little at this and they trooped into Davidson's bedroom.

The usual Babel of murmurs about the choice of word arose. Simpkins cut the discussion short.

"Of course, there's only one possible word – Zu-leika!"

"Two syllables or three?" asked Hawkins.

"Oh, don't bother about details now. Let's find some costumes."

Davidson's wardrobe was ransacked.

"Now, for the first syllable – " Simpkins began.

Heavy footsteps were heard and then a knock at the door.

"You can't come in here. We're dressing up," shouted Simpkins.

"Is Mr Hawkins there?" said a voice.

Hawkins opened the door and found himself facing the college porter.

"I'm sorry to disturb your party, Sir, but the Proctor's down below. He wants to know if there's a Miss Dobson with you."

Hawkins looked embarrassed.

"Tell him to come up," said Simpkins, "tell him he's just in time for the fun, tell him he can choose what part he likes, tell him – "

"Very good, Sir," said the porter.

Mackenzie arrived.

"Hello, Mac," cried Simpkins, "you're just in time for a little green room gossip. Come and help me to dress as the King of Beasts."

Mackenzie blinked.

"I wish to see a Mr Hawkins," he said.

"No, you don't, Mac," said Simpkins. "What you've come for is to renew your acquaintance with Miss Dobson. Here she is, Mac, divinely beautiful and divinely ready to forgive you."

"Really," began Mackenzie, "I have no wish to intrude upon a private gathering, but in accordance with the Vice Chancellor's instructions I am obliged to – "

"Don't worry, Mac. You've nothing to do. I've made all the further enquiries myself. Now you go into the next room and help to swell the audience."

Mackenzie stared helplessly at the group of half-dressed figures. Hawkins came forward.

"Yes, do go in, Sir. You'll find Mr and Mrs Duxberry there."

So Mackenzie found himself talking politely to Mrs Duxberry about his plans for the Long Vacation and the vacant professorship of Hebrew and the forthcoming concert of the Fugue Society and other seasonable topics. In a few minutes they were watching the First Scene of the charade in which an August Personage, attended by her suite, was conducted round the Zoo to see a newly-arrived lion of great ferocity; the Second Scene in which the same Personage from a stand at Ditton Corner witnessed the sinking of a clinker four (it sank because it was a "leaker"); and the Final Scene in which the Personage, seated on an improvised throne and wearing an improvised crown, received the homage of her faithful subjects. Duxberry and his wife applauded in rapture, and Mackenzie clapped uncomfortably.

"I think perhaps," he said, "that I had better be going now. It is clearly not an appropriate time for the discussion of official business."

"Of course it isn't," said Simpkins. "*Dulce est desipere*, Mac, and we're certainly *in loco* to-night."

"I'm glad we didn't have to play the charade in Latin," said Zuleika to Mrs Duxberry.

"Ah, these classical dons," said Mrs Duxberry indulgently, "it's second nature to them, I suppose."

"Well, second nature's better than original sin," retorted Simpkins. "Don't you think so, Miss Dobson?"

"I prefer Art to both," said Zuleika.

"I'm bound to say that I agree with Miss Dobson, " said Mackenzie, unexpectedly.

"Of course you do, Mac," said Simpkins. "Miss Dobson," he went on, turning to Zuleika, "we have an institution in Cambridge known as May Week. As many commentators have explained, it isn't exactly a week and it isn't in May, but it can be quite pleasant. Concerts, you know, and balls and boat-races, and – "

"I know," said Zuleika quietly.

"Well, a sister-in-law of mine is bringing a few friends this year to be my guests. Couldn't I induce you to join us?"

Zuleika pondered. She had to confess to herself that the evening had been enjoyable, though she did not quite know why. To be admired and adored by men was nothing new to her; but Cambridge men gave no sign of wanting to lie down and die for love of her. Instead, they stood about and made harmless jokes. Zuleika still knew what she liked; and she was growing a little tired of innocent fun.

"Who'll have some Moselle cup?" said Hawkins, from the other end of the room.

"All of us," shouted Simpkins, "except Mackenzie. He'd prefer a whiskey and soda."

"Simpkins," said Mackenzie, embarrassed, "you might at least let me state my own preferences."

"Certainly, Mac. Just tell Miss Dobson how much you'd prefer it if she came for May Week."

"Of course," said Mackenzie, still more confused, "but it's hardly for me to…"

Zuleika came to his rescue.

"Thank you," she said slowly. "It has certainly been interesting to learn something of Cambridge. But Mr Mackenzie need have no fear; I should not dream of bringing fresh embarrassment upon his Syndicate."